Petra, Mother, & Father

The Farm

Petra & Mother

Mother Schmidt

Kisses from Rosa

by Petra Mathers

An *Apple Soup* Book   *An Imprint of Alfred A. Knopf • New York*

For Mami and Papi

APPLE SOUP IS A TRADEMARK OF ALFRED A. KNOPF, INC.
Text and illustrations copyright © 1995 by Petra Mathers

Library of Congress Cataloging-in-Publication Data
Mathers, Petra.
Kisses from Rosa / by Petra Mathers.
p.   cm.
An Apple Soup Book.
Summary: While her mother is treated for a serious illness, Rosa stays with
her aunt and cousin on a farm in the Black Forest.
ISBN: 0-679-82686-6 (trade) — ISBN: 0-679-92686-0 (lib. bdg.)
[1. Farm life—Fiction. 2. Mothers and daughters—Fiction.]
I. Title
PZ7.M423933Ki   1995
[Fic]—dc20   94–32500

Manufactured in Singapore
2 4 6 8 0 9 7 5 3 1

Book design by Edward Miller

Dear Reader,

When I was Rosa's age, the worst thing that could happen was for my mother to go away. Yet that is exactly what she did—often, and for months on end. She had tuberculosis, which took a long time to heal.

The words "Mami has to go away" always took the bottom out from under me. The first days after she was gone, I seesawed between tears and giggles. I was sick from missing her, but also excited by this different life without her. In time I got used to it, but I often imagined her watching me or waiting for me, and that was very comforting.

The most memorable time was when I was sent off to Aunt Mookie and Birgit in the Black Forest. That was in 1949, barely four years after the war. My father was struggling to take care of "his two ladies"; I hardly ever saw him. What I remember most about him during those years is that he also cried when my mother left.

When you love someone and they go away, it leaves a hole in you. Even if you know that they'll be coming back, it hurts just the same. This story is for all of you.

Petra Mathers

It was quiet in the Black Forest. Mr. Kugel drove his taxi through the night. In the back seat, his small passenger had cried herself to sleep. Her name was Rosa, and she was going to her aunt's house, far from home in the city.

The reason for this visit was a noise…a whistling noise. Rosa's mother had it in her lungs. The doctor had sent her to a special hospital high up in the mountains, where the air was light and clean. There she could rest and get well.

"My favorite person will be the mailman because he will bring me your letters," said Rosa's mother when she kissed her daughter good-bye.

Later that night, Rosa felt herself lifted from the car, carried inside, and placed under warm covers.

She woke to a rooster crowing *kikeriki* right below her window. Across from her slept a tall girl with long hair and pink cheeks. Rosa stretched to see better. Why, she barely fit into this tiny bed. She was in a crib!

Rosa's mother would never have put her into a baby bed. What was her mother doing now? Was she thinking of Rosa?

A big tear rolled down Rosa's cheek.

"Mama, Mama! She's awake." The tall girl was sitting up blinking.

A lady in a pink nightgown sailed in.

"Good morning and welcome," she sang, pulling Rosa close through the bars. "I'm your Aunt Mookie, my goodness, you're much too big for this crib, but it's our only extra bed, how about waffles for breakfast, and you and Birgit can give Clara her morning milk, stand up straight, Birgit."

Rosa had never heard anyone speak so fast. But yes, she would like some waffles. And yes, she would like to give Clara some milk. And *now* she remembered Birgit, whom she'd met long ago when she was only three and Birgit was six.

Today was Birgit's last day of school before summer vacation. After breakfast she slipped a satchel over her shoulders and the two girls stepped into the crisp morning air.

A funny little dog, tail wagging, ears flapping, ran toward them. "Oh, look, a sausage on legs," laughed Rosa, and bent down to pet him.

"That's Waldi, the best dog in the Whole Wild World," Birgit called over her shoulder, and was gone.

Aunt Mookie helped Rosa unpack her suitcase. It smelled of home inside. Rosa's lower lip began to tremble.

"Look at these pretty sandals," Aunt Mookie said, kneeling down beside her. "And what might be in this little box?"

"My lady cards," sniffled Rosa. "Every time Mami buys margarine there is a picture inside. See, on the back it tells you what this lady might be thinking."

"'*When a woman says no, she means perhaps,*'" Aunt Mookie read, and laughed. "When I say no, I *mean* no."

"That's what Mami says too," giggled Rosa.

Rosa and Aunt Mookie fluffed up the feather beds and hung them out the window. "Tonight you'll smell the sunshine when you go to sleep," said Aunt Mookie.

When Birgit came home from school, her satchel and arms were stuffed with books. "Look, Rosa, this one is about a girl who lives by herself because her papa is a sea captain. And this is about a little boy with a wooden horse, and when he dies…"

"Oh, my darling bookworm," Aunt Mookie laughed, "not now. Outside, outside, the sun is shining."

Birgit sighed, peering at Rosa through her thick, round glasses. Her eyes looked as if they were floating in little lakes. "Let's visit the cows," she said, and took her cousin by the hand.

On their way, they saw a couple sitting on a bench.

"The Schmidts," said Birgit. "They own this farm."

"What's the matter with his leg?" whispered Rosa.

"It's wood. He left his real leg in the war," Birgit whispered back.

"Oh, the poor man, does it hurt?" cried Rosa.

"This thing? Not a bit," answered Mr. Schmidt. "Watch." And he picked up a stick and snapped it neatly in half over his wooden leg.

"Couldn't do without him for kindling," chuckled his wife, who was plucking a chicken. "Call me Mother Schmidt, sweetheart," she said, and held out a feathery hand. Rosa didn't feel like shaking hands just then, so she gave her an extra-friendly smile instead.

When they opened the stable door, all the cows turned and stared, then continued munching. Swallows swooped in and out the window; chickens and ducks snoozed on bales of hay. A gigantic rooster, standing on one leg, jerked his head this way and that. When he looked at Rosa sideways, the red flap under his beak wiggled.

"Make him go away," she said under her breath.

"Shoo, Josef!" And squawking and fluttering like an excited chicken, Birgit chased him out the door.

So summer on the farm began. The sun shone day after day, and the blueberries in the woods turned from green to pale purple to deep blue.

One morning, when Rosa and Aunt Mookie were hanging laundry, Mother Schmidt walked by. "Berries must be just about ripe now," she said, swinging her bucket. "Anyone want to come?"

Rosa ran off to fetch a pot.

As they walked up the path, clouds of dust puffed up behind them.

"You could fry eggs on the roof today," groaned Mother Schmidt, and rolled down her stockings. Before them were the first patches of berries, warm and juicy. Rosa picked one for the pot, one for the mouth, one for the mouth, one for the pot. When she noticed the bottom of Mother Schmidt's bucket was already covered, she picked one for the pot, one for the pot, one for the mouth.

Her hands were sticky; flies buzzed around her. She stood and stretched.

"Mother Schmidt," she yelled, "there are huge yellow things on your back!"

"Hornets," said Mother Schmidt. "If we don't scare them, they won't sting. They'll just think I'm a giant blueberry."

Back at home, Aunt Mookie was proud of Rosa's potful of berries. "When we make jam, we'll put stickers on the jars that say 'Rosa's Blueberry Delight.'"

It wasn't long before Rosa and Otto, the mailman, became good friends. When Otto had a letter from her mother, he waved it above his head as he bicycled down the path. Sometimes he wouldn't bring one for days, and Rosa's face would grow longer and longer. Otto would feel around inside his bag to make absolutely sure he hadn't overlooked anything. Often he found a gumdrop or jawbreaker. He'd hand it to Rosa, sniff the air, and say:

"No reason for tears, no reason for sorrow,
I can tell by the breeze, there'll be a letter tomorrow."

On Sundays, Rosa wrote to her mother. First she painted pictures of all the things that had happened. Then she sat on Aunt Mookie's lap.

"Dear Mami," they wrote, Aunt Mookie guiding Rosa's hand:

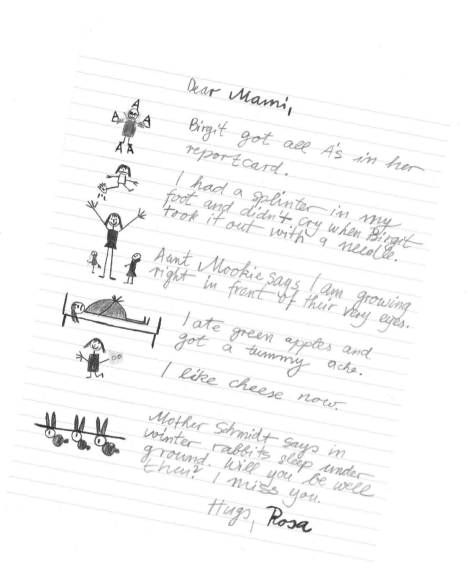

Dear Mami,

Birgit got all A's in her reportcard.

I had a splinter in my foot and didn't cry when Birgit took it out with a needle.

Aunt Mookie says I am growing right in front of their very eyes.

I ate green apples and got a tummy ache.

I like cheese now.

Mother Schmidt says in winter rabbits sleep under ground. Will you be well then? I miss you.

Hugs, Rosa

In every letter she sent a kiss.

"Here is an Eskimo kiss. It's flying up the mountain to rub noses with you."

"Here is a bird kiss. It chirps and kisses at the same time."

"Here is a butterfly kiss. To send one back, just flutter your eyelashes."

Once she wrote on the envelope: "BEWARE, wet fish kiss inside."

And when she was in a hurry one day, she sent a throw kiss.

But the next time she carefully drew a lion kiss. "This one hurts just a little bit," she warned.

Her mother wrote back: "All your kisses are helping me to get better very quickly. The doctor says he can hardly hear the whistling noise anymore. Maybe we'll be together for Christmas."

Slowly the days got shorter. The air was hazy and smelled of apples. Every year the best ones were stored in the root cellar. While Rosa arranged them on the shelves, Mother Schmidt grunted under the weight of basket after basket full of apples. "You take it easy down there, Mother," called Mr. Schmidt, fidgeting at the cellar door. "The world wasn't made in one day."

"Oh, hush," puffed Mother Schmidt. "I've got myself a great helper. Right, Rosa?"

"Right," answered Rosa proudly.

The weather grew cold and wet, the wind rattling around the house at night. There were always socks and boots drying by the stove. The family spent more and more time inside. So did the mice. Clara the cat would open one eye to watch them scurry from cupboard to cupboard, then doze off again.

Birgit did her homework at the kitchen table.

"Sit up straight, dear," Aunt Mookie said now and then, looking up from her sewing.

Rosa played on the floor. She liked to build towns with rivers and bridges. Her bear was the mayor, and she was a princess who lived in a castle high up in the mountains. Sometimes the mayor would send a telegram: "Urgent. STOP. Come now. STOP. Invaded by mice. STOP."

Then Rosa would lean books against the cupboard legs. The mice were trapped, the town was saved.

"Do you have my math book and ruler down there? I need them, please," Birgit would say.

In the early morning chill, Aunt Mookie rekindled the fire as Birgit and Rosa got dressed. They ate their breakfast around the stove.

Otto wore a slicker and earmuffs.

One day he brought a large, floppy envelope. "DO NOT BEND," he shouted from the top of the hill.

Inside Rosa found an Advent calendar with a note from her mother. "When you open the window with the 20 on it, Mr. Kugel will come and bring you home."

Home for Christmas! Rosa squeezed Aunt Mookie and Clara, then burst out the door. "Home for Christmas!" she sang, skipping around the house, Waldi yapping at her heels.

"Home for Christmas!" Mother Schmidt shouted, flinging her kitchen window open.

"Home for Christmas!" yodeled Mr. Schmidt, swinging his ax high at the woodpile.

That afternoon Aunt Mookie started her Christmas baking.

She rolled out the dough, and Rosa and Birgit cut out the shapes—a heart, an apple, and a dog. The dog was the hardest because his tail kept breaking off.

After the cookies cooled, Aunt Mookie put them in tin boxes. But they ate the dogs with the broken tails for dessert.

And then it began to snow. And snow. And snow. Inside the house the sounds were muffled. Rosa thought it was like living inside a giant cotton ball.

Birgit came home with a wreath she'd made in school on her head. It had four candles on it, one for each week before Christmas. "I couldn't hold it any longer," she moaned. "My hands are freezing."

Aunt Mookie gently picked the gloves off her fingers, and Rosa blew on them one by one. "Want to see what's in my Advent calendar's window today?" she asked.

Birgit laughed. "But we already peeked last night, silly. It's a shepherd."

From then on they practiced for the special good-bye concert they were planning by candlelight.

On Rosa's last night, Aunt Mookie and Birgit put on their best dresses. They had invited the Schmidts for cookies and hot chocolate.

"I'm an angel straight from heaven," announced Rosa as she climbed on a chair in her nightgown, with wings fastened to her back.

Aunt Mookie hummed the first bars of "Hark! The Herald Angels Sing," and everyone joined in.

Rosa had painted pictures for everyone, and they all had presents for her. Mother Schmidt had knitted Rosa red mittens with blue thumbs. Mr. Schmidt had carved a wooden Waldi. Aunt Mookie gave her a tin of cookies and a jar of Rosa's Blueberry Delight to take to her mother. And Birgit had made a shiny star for her Christmas tree back home.

Then it was time for bed. Rosa's last night in the crib.

Tomorrow her mother would tuck her into her own bed back in the city.

She closed her eyes and imagined her mother.

"Tomorrow," she whispered.

When Mr. Kugel arrived at dawn, it was still snowing. "Don't worry," he assured Aunt Mookie. "My auto takes to snow like a duck to water."

Rosa, Birgit, and Aunt Mookie huddled together in one big hug. Rosa gave Aunt Mookie a fierce lion kiss and Birgit a special good-bye kiss smack on the nose.

"Stand up straight, dear," Rosa teased between tears.

"Off you go, be good."

With Waldi barking and everyone waving, the taxi disappeared behind the snowflakes.

"Here," said Mr. Kugel, handing Rosa his handkerchief. "Now stop that sniffling and tell me what you've been up to all this time."

Rosa blew her nose. "Did you know swallows live in barns?" she asked him. "And hornets don't sting if you don't scare them? And kisses can make you well?"